NICKI MINAJ

Stuart A. Kallen

ReferencePoint
Press

San Diego, CA

About the Author

Stuart A. Kallen is the author of more than 350 nonfiction books for children and young adults. He has written on topics ranging from the theory of relativity to the art of electronic dance music. In 2018 Kallen won a Green Earth Book Award from the Nature Generation environmental organization for his book *Trashing the Planet: Examining the Global Garbage Glut*. In his spare time he is a singer, songwriter, and guitarist in San Diego.

For more information, contact:
ReferencePoint Press, Inc.
PO Box 27779
San Diego, CA 92198
www.ReferencePointPress.com

LIBRARY OF CONGRESS CATALOGING-IN-PUBLICATION DATA

Names: Kallen, Stuart A., 1955– author.
Title: Nicki Minaj/by Stuart A. Kallen.
Description: San Diego: ReferencePoint Press, 2019. | Series: Giants of
 Rap and Hip-Hop | Includes bibliographical references and index. |
 Audience: Grades 10-12
Identifiers: LCCN 2019037541 (print) | LCCN 2019037542 (ebook) | ISBN
 9781682827819 (library binding) | ISBN 9781682827826 (ebook)
Subjects: LCSH: Minaj, Nicki—Juvenile literature. | Rap musicians—United
 States—Juvenile literature.
Classification: LCC ML3930.M313 K35 2019 (print) | LCC ML3930.M313
 (ebook) | DDC 782.421649092 [B]—dc23
LC record available at https://lccn.loc.gov/2019037541
LC ebook record available at https://lccn.loc.gov/2019037542

Contents

CONTENTS

SPEARHEADING A MOVEMENT

Nicki Minaj is an American success story. She was born into poverty in Trinidad in 1982 and grew up poor in New York City. But Minaj single-mindedly developed her talents and rose out of poverty. She went on to make an indelible mark on hip-hop as a chart-topping rapper, business mogul, and international celebrity.

As one of the world's most successful hip-hop artists, Minaj has racked up a number of firsts. In 2010 Minaj was the first female rapper to perform a concert at Yankee Stadium in New York City. Two years later she was the first female rapper to perform at the Grammy Awards show. Minaj is the first female performer of any genre to chart one hundred *Billboard* Hot 100 hits. And in 2013 Minaj became the first woman to appear on the *Forbes* Hip Hop Cash Kings list, which tallies the net worth of popular rappers. Minaj explains the key to her success: "I've never been afraid to walk into the boy's club. *Ever*. Ever, ever, ever. . . . I kind of think of myself almost like a man. I'm not going to fall back from something because it's never been done before by a woman."[1]

Encouraging Women

From her first collection of songs, or mixtape, in 2007 to her 2018 chart-topping album *Queen*, Minaj has blazed her own trail through hip-hop culture. As she reminded fans in a 2019 Instagram post, "12 years ago I dropped my 1st mixtape. Wrote every single word on every single song. I was so proud of that."[2] Minaj's lyrics are filled with sarcasm and wordplay, and her vocals even adopt playful British and Jamaican accents on occasion. And with fifteen years of

4

formal vocal training, Minaj's ability to hit the high notes rivals any pop star.

Like many rappers, Minaj loves to brag about her sex appeal, her money, and her fame. But she also uses her fearless raps to take on issues such as racial injustice, poverty, and the difficulty of meeting society's beauty ideals. On social media Minaj offers positive messages for young women, encouraging fans to maintain close family ties and develop a good self-image. In 2017 she spoke out about the long-term problem of gender inequality in the music business: "Women must work TWICE as hard to even get HALF the respect her male counterparts get. When does this stop?"[3] Minaj went on to point out that she does not get the same level of recognition as male rappers and few men want to collaborate with her. She also scolded male rappers like Kendrick Lamar, Drake, and J. Cole for sexist comments they made about her and others.

> "I'm not going to fall back from something because it's never been done before by a woman."[1]
>
> —Nicki Minaj

Stirring Controversy

While some believe Minaj is a feminist icon, others criticize her for exploiting female sexuality to sell records and promote her brand. Minaj has also drawn fire for inciting feuds with notable pop stars and hip-hop artists. These beefs, which play out on Twitter and other social media sites, are always with women. Taylor Swift, Miley Cyrus, Remy Ma, and Cardi B are among those who have made Minaj's diss list. And Minaj encourages her rabid fan base—known as the Barbz—to post snarky comments about the competition on Twitter and Instagram. But Minaj knows controversy sells records and keeps her name trending.

Minaj's larger-than-life personality allows her to break barriers in an industry in which sexuality is rewarded and talent is often overlooked. And despite her hip-hop feuds, Minaj urges her fans to support other women, as she made clear in 2010: "I always wanted to be someone who spearheaded a movement, not just did something that worked for me. I want to get girls excited about being female rappers again and knowing that they can be kooky, goofy, playful, serious, hardcore—whatever it is, but you have the choice now."[4]

There is no argument that Minaj has spearheaded a movement that appeals to a vast audience. She can present herself as

Hip-hop superstar Nicki Minaj performs at the MTV Europe Music Awards. Although she is sometimes criticized for exploiting female sexuality in order to sell records, Minaj uses social media to offer positive messages for young women.

a ferocious political rapper, a friendly girl next door, a life-size Barbie doll, or a glammed-up sex symbol. With a net worth of over $85 million, Minaj has been many things to many people, and she shows other women—and women rappers—that they, too, do not have to embrace a single image. Whether she comes across as progressive or petty, playful or serious, her music speaks for itself. When the latest celebrity battle is forgotten, Minaj will already be in the record books as one of the world's most influential rappers. With her hot-pink wigs and bawdy lyrics, Minaj kicked open the door for a new generation of female hip-hop artists. As an immigrant who faced many hardships growing up, Minaj beat the odds by embracing the ideals of freedom, equality, and opportunity that define the American dream.

CHAPTER ONE

THE RAP QUEEN FROM QUEENS

Carol and Robert Maraj lived in a crowded house in Port of Spain, the capital city of the Republic of Trinidad and Tobago. Around fifteen adults, half a dozen children, and several pets lived in the three-room house, which belonged to Carol's mother. The house grew even more crowded when Onika Tanya Maraj was born on December 8, 1982. The little girl, called Nicki by friends and family, was the middle child of five. She had an older brother named Jelani and an older sister named Maya. A younger brother, Micaiah, and a younger sister, Ming, came along later. Today Nicki Maraj is known to the world as hip-hop superstar Nicki Minaj.

Carol and Robert did not have a happy marriage. Robert was jealous and abusive, as Carol recalled in 2012:

> If I only looked at someone it was an argument. If we went out I couldn't dance with anyone. If someone who knew me saw me out in the street and I spoke to that person it was a big argument and curse out in the street. . . . I was [twenty years old] when the abuse started.[5]

Carol put the needs of her children first and tried to make the best of the situation. She worked as a payroll and accounting clerk until she saved enough money to move to New York City when she was twenty-four. Robert did not want to leave Trinidad but followed Carol to New York six months later.

Carol and Robert settled in the Bronx borough of New York. Nicki and her siblings were left behind at their grandmother's house in Trinidad. During the two years that followed, Nicki mostly communicated with her parents by telephone. There were scenes of heartbreak when Carol came back to Port of Spain on vacation. At the end of each of her mother's visits, Nicki would get dressed, pack a small bag, and patiently stay up all night. As she later explained, "I would sit there and wait for her to leave, [thinking] that if she sees that I'm dressed, she'll take me with her."[6] On one occasion, four-year-old Nicki wrote a short song in which she said her mother took a piece of her away every time she left. Carol later said that, after hearing the song, she cried the entire six-hour flight back to New York.

Praying for Her Mother's Safety

Despite their rocky relationship, Carol and Robert worked hard to reunite their family, and things went well for a time. Robert got a good job, and with the financial help of Carol's father, they bought a house in the Queens borough. In 1988 five-year-old Nicki boarded an airplane with her brother and mother and flew to New York. The little girl had seen a lot of American television shows

Port of Spain, the capital of the island nation of Trinidad and Tobago, was home to Nicki Minaj until she moved to New York City at the age of five.

and thought she would be moving into a nice house with a big green lawn in the suburbs. The dangerous, crime-ridden South Jamaica neighborhood of Queens that her family called home was nothing like the images in her mind. Minaj later said that drug dealers hung out on the corner by her house. At that time New York and other big cities were flooded with a type of cheap, smokable cocaine called crack, which can make users manic and aggressive. The drug is highly addictive, and desperate crack users will sometimes lie, steal, and resort to violence to get another dose.

> "[When I was young] I would go in my room and kneel down at the foot of my bed and pray that God would make me rich so that I could take care of my mother."[7]
>
> —Nicki Minaj

Shortly after Minaj arrived in New York, her father became a crack addict. He lost his job and heaped abuse on Carol, flying into rages when she had no money to give him. Robert sold off the furniture and other family possessions, punched holes in walls, and terrorized the family. In a 2010 *Rolling Stone* interview, Minaj explained how she dealt with the trauma:

> When I first came to America I would go in my room and kneel down at the foot of my bed and pray that God would make me rich so that I could take care of my mother. Because I always felt like if I took care of my mother, my mother wouldn't have to stay with my father. . . . We didn't want him around at all, and so I always felt like being rich would cure everything, and that was always what drove me.[7]

One winter night Robert was on a crack binge when he tried (and failed) to burn down the house with Carol inside. After the incident Minaj had reoccurring nightmares about her father killing her mother. Sometimes when her parents were arguing, Minaj would stand in front of her mother with her hands on her hips in a meager attempt to protect her.

Robert eventually entered a drug-treatment program, stopped using drugs, and renewed his religious faith. Carol and Robert stayed together and were still married in 2019. While Robert is ashamed of his past, he was unhappy when Minaj described him as an unhinged crack fiend in the 2008 song "Autobiography." But as Minaj told *Rolling Stone*, "It's the price you pay when you abuse drugs and alcohol. Maybe one day your daughter will be famous and talk to every magazine about it, so think about that, dads out there who want to be crazy."[8]

Creating Drama

Minaj escaped from her chaotic reality by developing a rich imagination. From the age of nine, she was obsessed with hairstyling. Minaj later recalled what she told a neighbor who asked her why

Rappers from Queens

Rap music was born in the Bronx borough in New York City in the late 1970s. But the Queens borough produced some of hip-hop's biggest stars, including Nicki Minaj. One of Minaj's earliest influences was LL Cool J, who grew up in the Hollis neighborhood in Queens. LL Cool J, who has sold over 12 million records, was one of the first rappers to achieve mainstream success with the 1985 album *Radio*.

Queens was also home to Run-DMC, a seminal hip-hop group that provided inspiration to many rappers, including Minaj. Run-DMC crossed over into the pop charts in 1986 with a remake of the 1975 rock song "Walk This Way" by the group Aerosmith. Run-DMC also exerted a strong influence on hip-hop fashion, dressing in gold chains, black jeans, leather jackets, and fedora hats.

The hip-hop trio Salt-N-Pepa is another prominent rap act from Queens. Rappers Cheryl "Salt" James, Sandra "Pepa" Denton, and Deidra "DJ Spinderella" Roper founded the first all-female rap group in 1985. Salt-N-Pepa mixed big beats with brash feminist rhymes that took on male rappers with bravado. No one knows why Queens has produced so many rap stars, but the numbers prove that the borough is a hip-hop leader.

As a child, Nicki Minaj was obsessed with hairstyling, and even today she performs wearing wild wigs.

she brushed gobs of gel into her hair: "I never forget what I said: 'I'm someone new in this hair.'"[9] That early revelation stayed with Minaj, who still maintains a collection of wild wigs in the colors of the rainbow, ranging from hot pink and aqua to black-and-gold leopard spots.

The nutty vocalizations heard on Minaj's hit records are also built on fantasies she spun as a kid. From an early age Minaj invented characters that conversed in funny or odd voices. She incorporated them into the first rap songs she wrote and performed at age twelve after hearing an older neighbor girl making up hip-hop lyrics. Minaj also learned to play music; she was a good clarinet player in elementary school.

Minaj's creative instincts served her well when she entered the seventh grade at Elizabeth Blackwell Middle School in Queens. Her favorite class was English; the teacher encouraged students to write and act out plays based on their personal experiences. Minaj's contribution to a play called *Keeping the Peace* earned praise from her English teacher and even from the school principal. But Minaj was the kind of impulsive teenager that drives teachers crazy. Perhaps imitating the behavior she saw at home, Minaj would sometimes get into hair-pulling, clothes-ripping, face-scratching fights with other girls.

Becoming Harajuku Barbie

In 2007 when Nicki Minaj recorded her first mixtape, *Playtime Is Over*, she worked for months to compose lyrics and ensure every word was in the proper place. Even as she spent her days writing songs, Minaj knew she had to develop an over-the-top image that would attract clicks, likes, and shares from female fans on social media. That inspired Minaj to step into the role of a hip-hop doll she called Harajuku Barbie. As Minaj told MTV, "We're going with the whole Barbie doll theme. . . . I have to look like a doll straight out the box. But I'm not a Barbie that needs to play—*Playtime Is Over*." Minaj amplified the Barbie brand on the *Playtime Is Over* cover artwork. She posed with bright pink lipstick in what appears to be a plastic package that might hold a toy doll.

Today Minaj's most dedicated fans are referred to as Barbz, in reference to the Harajuku Barbie image. The female superfan Barbz of all ages try to dress like Minaj and obsess over her every comment on Twitter. Male fans, who wear short pink wigs, are known as Kens, named for the doll that is Barbie's boyfriend.

Quoted in Nadeska Alexis, "Nicki Minaj Channels Barbie in 'Playtime Is Over' Mixtape Shoot," MTV, April 4, 2012. www.mtv.com.

Despite her problems, Minaj cultivated her talents. By the time she graduated middle school, she was an accomplished singer, clarinetist, and actor. This qualified her to audition for a spot at the prestigious Fiorello H. LaGuardia High School of Music & Art and Performing Arts in Manhattan. LaGuardia is famous for producing notable actors, including Robert De Niro, Al Pacino, Jennifer Aniston, and Sarah Michelle Gellar. It was featured in the celebrated 1980 musical drama *Fame* about a group of artistic teens struggling to pursue music, art, and drama. (A remake of the movie was released in 2009.)

Minaj loved the idea of attending LaGuardia because she could sing all day long. She was a big fan of pop singers like Diana Ross and Cyndi Lauper and rapper Lauryn Hill, and she hoped to emulate their success stories. However, when Minaj went with her mother to the singing audition in 1996, she had a sore throat and her tryout went badly. Minaj was embarrassed and wanted to go

Nicki Minaj was a huge fan of pop singer Cyndi Lauper, shown here performing in 1986.

home, but her mother forced her to take the drama audition. The drama department at the school is extremely difficult to get into, but Minaj shone during her audition; she said the moment she got onstage, she felt like she was born to be there.

Minaj fit right in with the other artistic kids at LaGuardia, but her bad-girl attitude and desire to be the center of attention were apparent to all. As an unnamed classmate remembers,

> Her friends were kind of like the mean girls. You got the sense when you walked past her that she was talking about you or had some kind of joke going on. . . . You could tell at LaGuardia what someone's major was based on their behavior, and Nicki was definitely a drama major.[10]

With her flair for drama, Minaj transformed her image. When she started LaGuardia, she wore the popular styles of the era: Boss designer jeans and baggy Tommy Hilfiger shirts. However, after observing some of the glamorous teachers at the school, Minaj began wearing makeup, high heels, and fashionable skirts.

Struggling to Survive

LaGuardia attracts show business talent scouts, who are always searching for the next big star. (Talent scouts introduce actors and musicians to producers, directors, and other decision makers in the entertainment industry.) Again, Minaj had little trouble attracting attention. After performing at the school's final showcase, she was approached by ten scouts who wanted to work with her.

After graduating from high school in 2000, Minaj discovered that acting jobs were hard to find, despite the promises of talent scouts. And she needed a job so she could afford to move into her own apartment. In 2001 Minaj began working at the Red Lobster restaurant in the Bronx, serving seafood for twelve dollars an hour. The pay was pretty good for the era—Minaj was able to lease a white BMW luxury sports car. But she hated the hard work of waitressing; the kitchen was hot, orders had to be served quickly, and customers were often impatient and rude. One time a customer stole Minaj's pen, which prompted her to chase him out to the parking lot. She pounded on his car window, stuck up her middle finger, and demanded her pen back. This proved to be Minaj's last night at the Red Lobster. In 2010 Minaj said she had been fired about fifteen times over the years for rude behavior. But she said the hardest part about being repeatedly fired was keeping her failures from her mother: "I never wanted to accept that I was not ready to live on my own. My mother would call. I would be like, 'Everything's great!' But I wouldn't have food in the refrigerator. I refused to ask for anything."[11]

While hopping from job to job, Minaj tried to keep her acting career alive. In 2001 she landed a role in the play *In Case You Forget*. This production was referred to as an Off-Broadway play, because it was performed in a small theater with fewer than five hundred seats.

Attracting Dirty Money

Actors in Off-Broadway plays do not earn much money, and Minaj quickly came to understand that acting was no way to escape poverty. And after being fired once again—this time from a position in an office—she swore she would rather be homeless than work another nine-to-five job. Minaj decided to become a rap star. At first she tried to gain experience by making music with some of the male amateur rappers in her neighborhood. However, they only wanted her to sing background choruses. As Minaj recalls, "I hated doing anything that made me seem like a girl at that time. I wanted to be as strong as the boys and as talented as them and I wanted to show them I could do what they did."[12]

Minaj knew she would have to work hard with a single-minded focus to gain acceptance in the male-dominated hip-hop industry. Inspired

"I wanted to be as strong as the boys and as talented as them and I wanted to show them I could do what they did."[12]

—Nicki Minaj

by New York–based rappers like LL Cool J, Run-DMC, Salt-N-Pepa, and Foxy Brown, Minaj spent hours turning her thoughts and experiences into rap lyrics. In order to record her music, she traded office work at a small production company for free studio time. Minaj learned how to record beats from music samples and create demo tracks that she could give to agents and record executives. During this period neighbors would often see Minaj driving around Queens in her BMW with the windows rolled down, blasting her thumping rap demos.

In 2002 Minaj got her first break. One of her demos caught the ear of a rapper and music producer named Lou$tar, leader of local rap quartet the HoodStars. At Lou$tar's request, Minaj joined the group and played some local gigs. Minaj did not view the HoodStars as a ticket to success. The group recorded five rap songs, including its one and only hit, "Don't Mess with It" (2004). The song was played on national television by a WWE wrestler named Victoria when she entered the ring.

Minaj continued to promote herself, posting tracks on Myspace, a social networking website that was extremely popular at the time. Minaj's Myspace tracks attracted a growing number of fans who downloaded her music. She retained fans by personally communicating with listeners on Myspace, Twitter, and other social media sites. In 2006 Minaj used her online contacts to organize a concert at a local club, which attracted a standing-room-only crowd.

Music fans were not the only ones following Minaj on Myspace. Minaj sent out friend requests to numerous music industry insiders. One of them was a producer named Fendi, chief executive officer of the Brooklyn-based label Dirty Money Entertainment. Fendi was well known among New York rappers as someone who was willing to help talented newcomers develop their act and get record contracts. Fendi loved Minaj and in 2007 signed her to a six-month contract with Dirty Money. She was still using her last name, Maraj, but Fendi convinced her to adopt the stage name Nicki Minaj.

Street Videos

Dirty Money was in the practice of promoting its rappers with a series of DVDs called *The Come Up* and *Smack DVD*. These promotional videos, which contained short clips of rappers, were sold by street vendors or handed out at concerts. Minaj was first featured in a video that was shot on the streets of Queens. She thanks her fans for their support and boldly informs them that she is the best female rapper in the game. Another video shows Minaj in the studio performing the 1994 song "Warning" by rapper the Notorious B.I.G. The gangsta rap song, filled with violent imagery, was a bold choice for a female rapper. The clip created a buzz for Minaj and helped her increase the size of her audience. Most importantly, the video got the attention of rap superstar Lil Wayne, who liked what he heard. Lil Wayne asked Minaj to contribute to his celebrated 2007 mixtape *Da Drought 3*, and in the studio the two rappers developed an instant chemistry. According to Minaj, "He's no-holds-barred when he raps, and I've always been like that. I bring sarcasm and comedy, which [Lil Wayne] connects with. I guess we both dare to be different."[13]

When Minaj released her first mixtape, *Playtime Is Over*, in 2007, Lil Wayne appeared as a guest. Minaj wrote all twenty tracks on *Playtime Is Over*, which showcases her tough-girl attitude. Minaj's complex wordplay is mind-boggling whether she is bragging about her beauty, rapping humorously in a British cockney accent, or insulting other rappers. Minaj backs her brilliant lyrics—or bars, in hip-hop slang—with samples from some of the biggest pop and rap hits, including "Upgrade U" by Beyoncé and Jay-Z, "Can't Stop, Won't Stop" by Young Gunz, and "We Takin' Over" by DJ Khaled.

Minaj's childhood talent for inventing alternative personalities, or alter egos, finds expression on *Playtime Is Over*. One of Minaj's most

> "[Lil Wayne's] no-holds-barred when he raps, and I've always been like that. I bring sarcasm and comedy. . . I guess we both dare to be different."[13]
>
> —Nicki Minaj

enduring characters, Harajuku Barbie, was invented during the *Playtime Is Over* sessions. (Harajuku is a famous shopping district in Tokyo that is known as the center of Japanese youth culture and fashion.) The bawdy Harajuku Barbie doll character dresses in revealing outfits, huge hoop earrings, and wild wigs. She is a girly girl who—like Minaj—loves hot pink, fun fashions, and torrid love affairs. When Minaj is rapping as Harajuku Barbie, she uses a soft, sweet, sensual voice.

By developing a memorable persona and backing it with talent and determination, Minaj became more than just another rapper. *Playtime Is Over* put the world on notice that a new female rapper was on the scene. With musical skills developed during her school years, Minaj made herself into an instant icon. She could spit out bars better than the best rappers in the business. And she proved that she was as strong—and gifted—as the boys.

CHAPTER TWO

IN THE PINK

Lil Wayne's rap career was taking off when he founded Young Money Entertainment in 2005. The record label formed the basis of a hip-hop collective—a group of up-and-coming rap musicians who supported one another and collaborated on one another's records. Lil Wayne's Young Money crew consisted of Drake, Tyga, Mack Maine, and others. In 2007, after Lil Wayne discovered Nicki Minaj rapping in Queens, he convinced her to join the Young Money crew and relocate to his hometown, Atlanta, Georgia.

Minaj was a welcome addition to the Atlanta music scene, and she regularly sold out popular hip-hop nightclubs. But Minaj was facing a dilemma typical for all women rappers. As hip-hop journalist Aaron Williams writes, "At the time [Minaj] was making her entry into hip-hop, [record executives] and major publications couldn't seem to get past female rappers' looks."[14]

Minaj knew she could flaunt her beauty and sexuality. But this posed a risk: she might be dismissed as a trivial talent. She could try another approach, presenting herself as a strong, socially conscious rapper who wrote bars with deep insight into the human condition. Rather than choose one direction, Minaj went both ways. When she released her second mixtape, *Sucka Free* (2008), it included serious, personal songs about her childhood, like "Autobiography," as well as sexually provocative tracks such as "Grindin'" and "Lollipop." Minaj further highlighted her duel personalities in her rapping style. She could shift from airy sweetness to a serious low growl in a single verse.

One of Minaj's famous alter egos, Nicki Lewinsky, made her first appearance on *Sucka Free*. The character was in-

Nicki Minaj performs onstage with rapper Lil Wayne (on right). In 2007, Minaj decided to move to Atlanta and join Wayne's hip-hop collective, Young Money Entertainment.

spired by Monica Lewinsky, who had an affair with President Bill Clinton while working in the White House in the mid-1990s. While many Americans were critical of Monica Lewinsky's behavior, Minaj's Nicki Lewinsky was a positive role model. Journalist Allison P. Davis explains, "[Nicki Lewinsky is] a sexual disrupter . . . a woman who knows the power of her own sexuality and can harness it for great wealth and, ultimately, power."[15]

Minaj's crazy characters, vocal acrobatics, and bad-girl bars earned respect from music critics. After releasing *Sucka Free*, Minaj was named Female Artist of the Year at the 2008 Underground Music Awards, a group that honors the achievements of independent urban artists who do not have record deals.

> "[Nicki Lewinsky is] a woman who knows the power of her own sexuality and can harness it for great wealth and, ultimately, power."[15]
>
> —Allison P. Davis, journalist

Putting the Music Front and Center

Minaj released her next mixtape, *Beam Me Up Scotty*, in April 2009. She said that with this new release, she wanted to focus on music rather than her image: "People knew me more for [sexy] pictures than my music. But with the *Beam Me Up Scotty* mixtape, they have to take me seriously as an artist. So . . . I started sharpening my skills. Recently, I've been singing more."[16]

Minaj's sharpened skills and improved vocals make *Beam Me Up Scotty* a standout mixtape. She took the name of the mixtape from a catchphrase inspired by the 1960s science fiction television show *Star Trek*. She played up the association on the mixtape cover art, which showed her dressed in a cartoonish superhero costume beneath a beam emanating from a spaceship.

Beam Me Up Scotty, which features guest verses by Young Money artists like Drake, Gudda Gudda, Jae Millz, Mack Maine, and Lil Wayne, was universally acclaimed by fans and critics. Minaj spits out her rapid-fire bars, sings sweetly on choruses featuring tight harmonies, and adds occasional humor by rapping in a singsong Jamaican accent. Williams describes Minaj's musical growth on *Beam Me Up Scotty*: "[Minaj] flashes all of the hallmarks of her signature style, but [uses her] characters and vocal quirks . . . to accentuate her delivery, turning what might ordinarily be clichéd brags and weather-worn flexes into sparkling displays of her sharp-tongued wit and wordplay."[17]

Minaj also trod new ground with the music on *Beam Me Up Scotty*. The samples on her previous mixtapes were lifted directly from hip-hop hits by Jay-Z, the Notorious B.I.G., and other best-selling rappers. But the backing music on the new mixtape had a creative new gloss, featuring radio-friendly flourishes like synthesizer crescendos, stinging rock guitar licks, and wavy, distorted vocals processed through Auto-Tune recording software. These additions came to define the successful sound Minaj would use in the future. Minaj's superfans—the Barbz—loved the new sounds and pushed the track "I Get Crazy" to number twenty on *Billboard*'s Hot Rap Songs chart.

When *Beam Me Up Scotty* dropped, Minaj had little competition from female rappers. Queen Latifah, the top female rapper in the 1990s, was focused on acting. Neither Lil' Kim nor Missy Elliott had released an album since 2005. Foxy Brown's last record, *Broken Silence*, was eight years old at the time. According to Williams, "There were very few albums out from serious female rappers. . . . The void for female voices [in 2009] was pressing and immediate, a vacuum into which Nicki Minaj injected a much-needed presence with her outsized persona and insane delivery."[18] Fans could also see Minaj live and hear her insane delivery on large tour stages. She displayed her rap skills at the Young Money Presents: America's Most Wanted Music Festival. The hip-hop festival played thirty-two cities in 2009 and featured other Young Money artists, including Drake, Young Jeezy, and Jeremih.

> "The void for female voices was pressing and immediate, a vacuum into which Nicki Minaj injected . . . her outsized persona and insane delivery."[18]
>
> —Aaron Williams, journalist

However crazy Minaj might have sounded on records, she proved herself as a savvy businesswoman when she signed a record deal with Young Money Entertainment in August 2009. The global music giant Universal Music Group is the parent company of Young Money, and Minaj negotiated herself a profitable deal. Oftentimes, major record labels persuade artists to give up the right to money earned from product promotions, public appearances, music publishing, and merchandise sales. In exchange, the labels promote an artist's records and help sponsor concert tours. But when Minaj signed with Young Money, she cemented a deal that allowed her to retain all rights to her music and image and received all money generated by her brand.

Ups and Downs

While many rappers dream of signing a contract with a major label, few consider the nonstop hard work required for success in the music business. By early 2010 Minaj was on an endless promotional tour, traveling relentlessly between concert stages, recording sessions, and television studios. She barely had time to eat and rarely slept more than four hours at night. On the upside, Minaj was the fastest-rising star in the music business. She made guest appearances on hit records by pop and hip-hop superstars, including Mariah Carey, Gucci Mane, Usher, Christina Aguilera, and Robin Thicke. Minaj's biggest accomplishment was a song-stealing guest appearance on Kanye West's "Monster."

Nicki Minaj in an appearance with rapper Kanye West, who noted her enormous potential as a hip-hop artist.

Minaj Is a Monster

In 2010 Kanye West was already considered one of the world's most innovative rappers when he released the controversial song "Monster." The single was from West's fifth album, *My Beautiful Dark Twisted Fantasy.* As the title indicates, "Monster" has a horror theme, with verses about ghouls, goblins, zombies, and murder. "Monster" features guest appearances by superstar rappers Jay-Z and Rick Ross. During the recording session, the rappers recommended Minaj to West. Minaj says she had been obsessed with Jay-Z since childhood and agreed to perform on the song just so she could meet him. When Minaj raps the final verse on "Monster," she steals the show, surpassing the performances of Jay-Z, Ross, and West. In the music press Minaj's verse about zombies eating brains was called fire-breathing, colossal, bonkers, and unhinged. The website HipHopDX named Minaj's turn Verse of the Year, while *Complex* magazine called it the Best Rap Verse of the Past 5 Years.

In the years since "Monster" was released, Minaj's iconic verse has been performed by a wide array of artists, including Ed Sheeran, Chloë Grace Moretz, and Demi Lovato. In 2016 the pop singer Adele famously rapped the verse on the popular "Carpool Karaoke" segment of *The Late Late Show with James Corden.*

After watching Minaj write and wickedly perform her verse for the song, West pointed out, "The scariest artist in the game right now is Nicki Minaj. She has the most potential out of everyone."[19] Every one of Minaj's guest appearances charted on the *Billboard* Hot 100. This made her the first female solo artist to have seven hits on this singles chart.

While Minaj was setting records working with others, she experienced a rare flop with one of her own songs. "Massive Attack," the lead single from her 2010 debut studio album, *Pink Friday*, was slammed by reviewers, and the track sold poorly. The song only reached number sixty-five on the Hot R&B/Hip-Hop Songs chart and

"The scariest artist in the game right now is Nicki Minaj. She has the most potential out of everyone."[19]

—Kanye West, rapper and producer

failed to chart at all on the *Billboard* Hot 100. "Massive Attack" was pulled from the *Pink Friday* album, putting more pressure on Minaj to ensure the upcoming album would break through to mainstream listeners. She had relocated to Los Angeles and spent most of her time in the studio, which she kept heated to a sweltering 90°F (32°C) because she believed the heat would help preserve her voice during long recording sessions.

While working to finish *Pink Friday*, Minaj felt that she needed to remain in the public eye. When Jay-Z and Eminem asked her to be the opening act on their Home & Home Tour, Minaj jumped at the chance. In September 2010 Minaj took the stage at a sold-out show at Yankee Stadium, making her the first female rapper to play at the famous baseball field.

When she was not touring or recording, Minaj spent her time studying the music industry. She was particularly interested in the convoluted methods devised by record labels to track sales of

"Massive Attack" Bombs

Nicki Minaj seemed to have a golden touch. She generated raves across the board for nearly every track that she produced. But in early 2010 Minaj slipped up with "Massive Attack," the lead single from her debut album, *Pink Friday*. Reviewers panned "Massive Attack," claiming the song did not live up to the standards of Minaj's earlier mixtapes. Many of the negative reviews centered on the "Massive Attack" video, which was shot in the desert northeast of Los Angeles. The video has a militaristic theme, with tanks, explosions, and car crashes. A pink Lamborghini sports car is chased by a helicopter speeding down a dirt road. Minaj changes costumes often and appears as a pink Harajuku Barbie, an anime soldier, and a bikini-clad jungle cat in a green wig. The video was supposed to introduce Minaj to a new audience and generate excitement for *Pink Friday*, but many found it difficult to follow the chaotic story the video was trying to tell. The "Massive Attack" fiasco left some in the hip-hop community wondering if Minaj was a fleeting talent who lacked staying power in a tough business.

music and merchandise. These complicated business practices are often used to cheat artists out of royalties, and Minaj was determined to get her fair share. She also took control of her image; she did her own styling for photo shoots and choreographed her dance moves when she appeared in videos. Ever the perfectionist, Minaj took her work seriously and expected those around her to do the same. "I push people around me but I don't push anyone more than I push myself," she says. "I tell people all the time, 'You want to work for me? You have to give 250,000%,' because when I'm in the [recording studio], I don't half-ass it. I demand perfection from everyone around me and if you can't live up to that, then bye-bye."[20]

While some found Minaj difficult to work with, she displayed a softer side when communicating with the Barbz online. Minaj's chart-topping guest appearances had pushed her Twitter account past 2 million followers. When she wanted to relax, she spent time communicating with her many fans. Minaj offered personal advice, positive reinforcement, and expressions of love to those struggling with poverty, addiction, and family problems. And she always told those who dreamed of success to pursue an education.

The Pink Party

Minaj's says her fan communications helped her understand what people wanted to hear: "I'm trying to make music for the masses. This is my chance to bring everyone into my party."[21] Fans were so excited to join Minaj's party that they began preordering *Pink Friday* six weeks before the album's release. This pushed it to number four on Amazon sales charts. When the highly anticipated album finally dropped in November, it debuted at number two on the *Billboard* 200, with sales totaling more than 385,000 the first week. *Pink Friday* soon hit number one on the US charts and was an international success, entering the top twenty in Canada, the United Kingdom, and Australia.

Pink Friday features collaborations with an illustrious cast of rap and pop megastars, including Eminem, Drake, Rihanna, will.i.am, and Kanye West. Minaj also performs as Harajuku Barbie and some crazy new characters. Roman Zolanski, described by Minaj as her gay male alter ego, raps angrily in a low, snarling British accent. Roman's mother, Martha Zolanski—supposedly Minaj's godmother—tells Roman to stop acting crazy. Nicki Lewinsky reappears, this time having an affair with a character called President Carter, played by Lil Wayne (whose real last name is Carter).

Pink Friday generated eight singles, including "Roman's Revenge," "Moment 4 Life," and "Fly." Some were released before the album dropped, while others were released in 2011 to keep *Pink Friday* on the charts. The biggest single from the album, "Super Bass," exemplified the playful pop-rap style that made *Pink Friday* unlike anything Minaj had ever recorded. "Super Bass" features electronic dance music synthesizers bubbling behind Minaj's mile-a-minute raps. Minaj also takes a turn as a pop vocalist, highlighting her singing talents on the infectious chorus.

The "Super Bass" video is saturated with Minaj's favorite color. Her troupe of Barbz dancers wear bubblegum-pink wigs and glow-in-the-dark pink lipstick. Minaj appears in a pink bodysuit with a giraffe print. The video also features a pink Ferrari sports car, a pink airplane, a swimming pool filled with pink water, and even pink cocktails. Minaj says she wanted to give her Barbz an extremely colorful video filled with eye candy, such as muscular male dancers in bathing suits. The "Super Bass" video was viewed over 787 million times on YouTube by 2019, and the single reached number three on the Hot 100. The song went on to sell over 8 million copies. Making the video was inspiring for Minaj, who says, "I would like to put out 50 videos. Videos really tell the story a lot more elaborately than just the song does."[22]

Focusing on Feminism

With *Pink Friday* generating intense interest, Minaj launched a new business venture. A week after the album dropped, Minaj released a lipstick called Pink 4 Friday. The limited-edition lipstick was only available online for four consecutive Fridays during the 2010 Christmas shopping season. Weekly allotments sold out quickly.

Lipstick was not the only product associated with Minaj. During the Halloween season, the Nicki Minaj costume, with a pink giraffe-print jumpsuit and platinum blonde wig, was a best seller. But after the success of *Pink Friday*, Minaj said she was trying to tone down her raunchy language and sexual posturing, especially at concerts, where some attendees brought their young children. Instead, Minaj wanted to promote a feminist message to her fans:

> I have the same power as these boys. . . . There's nothing different between me and them. . . . I no longer feel lesser than; I don't want my girls to feel that way. I want them to feel that, even if you have a nine-to-five [job], if you grow up to be vice president of the company, you should earn the same thing the male vice president earned. You should demand the same thing.[23]

Throughout 2011 Minaj continued to exhibit her power and earning potential. She promoted her latest singles at radio stations and played sold-out concerts across the country. Minaj joined singer Britney Spears's Femme Fatale Tour, and she released a remix of a Spears's single "Till the World Ends" with pop singer Kesha. The song peaked at number three on the Hot 100. In another high-profile collaboration, Minaj performed with music icon Prince at a Versace fashion show in New York City.

Not Taking Any Holidays

When the Grammy Awards were announced at the end of 2011, Minaj received three nominations: Best New Artist, Best Rap Performance by a Duo or Group (for "My Chick Bad" with Ludacris), and Best Rap Album. Minaj did not win any of the awards for which she was nominated, but she was the first solo female rapper ever to perform on the annual Grammy Awards show, held in February 2012. However, Minaj generated controversy when she walked the red carpet with an actor dressed as the pope. Minaj later played a new song, "Roman Holiday," while conducting a mock exorcism on a stage surrounded by half-naked dancers posing as choirboys and monks. A conservative

When Nicki Minaj appeared at the 2012 Grammy Awards with an actor dressed as the pope and conducted a mock exorcism, her performance was criticized as sacrilegious and lewd.

organization called the American Catholic League wrote that the performance was sacrilegious and called it lewd and insulting to religion.

Stirring up controversy might be one of Minaj's main fields of expertise, and her ability to rivet the public's attention helped her skyrocket to the top. But the key to her stardom could be traced to her willingness to focus on her goals and work extremely hard. And Minaj had a different definition of success than most. After the release of *Pink Friday*, she said she was not interested in using her money to relax on the beach or sit in a hot tub. Success to her meant being able to take care of her mother while putting her nieces through college. And as Minaj said, she was not about to put her feet up: "This is stressful, but I wouldn't trade it for the world. Sometimes you want to get a couple of extra hours of sleep, but this is just the beginning. We're just getting started."[24]

CHAPTER THREE

RACKING UP RECORDS

In February 2012 pop singer Madonna performed at what was then the most-watched television event in American history. Around 167 million people tuned in to the Super Bowl XLVI football game. During the halftime festivities, Madonna performed several songs, including her recent hit "Give Me All Your Luvin'." The single featured Nicki Minaj and rapper M.I.A. Both women rappers joined Madonna onstage for an extravagant performance that included dancing cheerleaders with pom-poms and a marching band. This was easily the most people Minaj had ever played to. But according to Minaj, performing for a huge audience was not the best part of the experience. Minaj recalls:

> Meeting Madonna changed my life. Working with Madonna changed my life. Rehearsing with Madonna for two weeks changed my life. . . . This is the first performance that I'm proud of in my entire career. I saw how much Madonna sacrificed and how much she rehearses and rehearses and rehearses and rehearses. . . . The Madonna situation inspired me to give it my all and put that work in.[25]

Touching the Sky

Minaj was being uncharacteristically humble—the twenty-nine-year-old rapper was no stranger to putting the work in. Immediately after the Super Bowl gig, she was back in the studio recording and producing her upcoming studio album *Pink Friday: Roman Reloaded*, scheduled for release in April

2012. The first single from the album, "Starships," dropped little more than a week after the dazzling Super Bowl spectacle. And the single's genre-breaking sound was unlike anything else on the radio. "Starships" begins as a hip-hop song with Minaj spinning out her trademark bars in double-quick time. The song hastily morphs into European dance-pop, a fist-pumping sound driven by synthesizers, earthshaking bass runs, and popping electronic drums. On the chorus lines about dancing with her hands so high

"Meeting Madonna changed my life. Working with Madonna changed my life. Rehearsing with Madonna for two weeks changed my life."[25]

—Nicki Minaj

Nicki Minaj performs with pop singer Madonna during halftime at the 2012 Super Bowl. Minaj later said that working with Madonna changed her life.

they touch the sky, Minaj proves she can compete with the best pop singers in the business.

Minaj's hard-core hip-hop fans might have been disappointed with her new dance-pop sound. But if record sales are any indication, those who love the dance-pop of Madonna, Britney Spears, and Lady Gaga were thrilled about Minaj's new direction. "Starships" was a chart-topping, record-setting success. The song made *Billboard* history by spending twenty-one consecutive weeks in the top ten on the Hot 100. "Starships" also landed in the top five on record charts in fifteen countries, from Australia to Switzerland. By the end of 2012, "Starships" had sold 7.2 million copies worldwide, making it one of the best-selling singles of all time.

"Starships" Goes Viral

Nicki Minaj has often said she enjoys creating over-the-top videos that are a treat for the eyes as well as the ears. And Minaj knows how to create viral video sensations through the use of vividly colored costumes, spectacular dance routines, crazy story lines, and fist-pumping choruses. The 2012 "Starships," which had racked up over 350 million YouTube views by 2019, exemplifies how Minaj's dancing, singing, and fantastic fashion create a link between the artist and her fans. The video begins with beautiful people in bathing suits lounging on a tropical island. Minaj, wearing a bubblegum-pink bikini and long greenish-blonde wig, is beamed into the scene as an alien coming down from a starship. She begins rapping, singing, and dancing as the islanders worship her as a goddess. Night falls as a spectacular glow-in-the-dark dance party begins, complete with tribal fire dancers and colorful kaleidoscopic special effects. The scenes are carefully crafted to portray Minaj as strong, sassy, confident, and otherworldly. While the dance routines are complicated, fans at home have worked out some of the steps and shared them with the world on YouTube. And the simple lyrics to the chorus can be shouted out even by those who might not be fluent in English.

Bad Bars and Bubblegum

"Starships" helped build excitement for the release of *Pink Friday: Roman Reloaded*. The album features collaborations with rappers Nas, Drake, and Lil Wayne, as well as with rhythm and blues (R&B) singer Chris Brown. When Minaj was asked in a Twitter forum to describe the new record in one word, she tweeted: "Freedom."[26] She later elaborated. Minaj explained that she felt the need to be guarded on her first studio album, avoiding vulgarity so she could make music that appealed to the widest audience. She also said some of the songs on *Pink Friday* were very personal, like opening her diary to the world. This time around, Minaj said she just wanted to have fun and feel free.

As the title *Pink Friday: Roman Reloaded* implies, Minaj's crazed alter ego Roman Zolanski was prominently featured on the album. The title track, "Roman Reloaded," which features verses by Lil Wayne, finds Minaj at her raunchy, unhinged best. Her bars recapture the outlandish outlook so often displayed on early mixtapes like *Beam Me Up Scotty*. The beats that drive "Roman Reloaded," which might be compared to beating on an aluminum trash can with a wrench, echo 1980s hard-core rap popularized by Run-DMC.

Minaj's throwback rap style can be heard on the first half of *Pink Friday: Roman Reloaded*. On the second half of the sixty-nine-minute album, Minaj is in mega-dance-pop mode with club anthems like "Pound the Alarm" and "Automatic." Minaj also explores her softer side for the first time with the introspective R&B ballads "Marilyn Monroe" and "Right by My Side."

Some in the music press derided the album's mix of musical styles as disjointed. But reviewer Jody Rosen had a different take:

> Nicki Minaj is a purist's nightmare. She doesn't just straddle pop categories, she dumps them in a Cuisinart [food processor], whips them to a frothy purée, then trains a

guided missile at the whole mess. She is a rapper's rapper, a master of flow and punch lines, with skills to please the most exacting gatekeepers of hip-hop street cred. But she's a bubblegum starlet as well, delivering confections to the nation's mall rats.[27]

As usual, Minaj's mall rats and Barbz loved the new music. *Pink Friday: Roman Reloaded* debuted at number one on the *Billboard 200*, and fans bought more than a quarter million copies of the album the first week. By the end of 2012, over 785,000 copies of the record had been purchased, making it the best-selling rap album of the year and the third-highest-selling R&B/hip-hop album. *Pink Friday: Roman Reloaded* also debuted at the top of the album charts in the United Kingdom and Canada. And the new album showed that Minaj was gaining on her mentor Madonna; the rise of *Pink Friday: Roman Reloaded* knocked Madonna's album *MDNA* off the top of the charts.

> "Nicki Minaj is a purist's nightmare. She doesn't just straddle pop categories, she dumps them in a Cuisinart [food processor], whips them to a frothy purée, then trains a guided missile at the whole mess."[27]
>
> —Jody Rosen, music reviewer

Two Pink Friday Tours

With the release of *Pink Friday: Roman Reloaded*, Minaj followed a pattern she had established with her first album. Rather than create new music, she continued to release singles from the album to keep her name at the top of the charts. Minaj also went on tour—her first time as a headliner rather than a warm-up act. Minaj's 2012 Pink Friday Tour lasted from May until August, playing forty-four cities in Australia, Japan, Europe, and North America. As reviewer Jon Caramanica wrote after seeing the Chicago performance, Minaj "inspires fervor [in her fans]. Even when she was on a slow simmer . . . her crowd was manic, vibrating, loose."[28]

The fan fervor was so intense that Minaj's Twitter feed was bombarded by Barbz requesting more concerts. This inspired Minaj to launch a second series of shows, the Pink Friday: Reloaded Tour, which hit eighteen cities in Europe, Oceania, and Asia between October and December. The tour was bigger, better, and more spectacular than the first go-round, or as Minaj describes it, like the "Pink Friday Tour on steroids."[29]

In between concerts, Minaj made her acting debut as the voice of Steffie in the animated film *Ice Age: Continental Drift*. Minaj says landing the role was a blessing and an honor, and she was thrilled to be costarring in the movie with Queen Latifah.

> "I've looked up to her for so many years, she embodies everything that I'd like to do, you know?" Minaj says. "She does acting, animation voices—she's everything to me. To be a part of something she's a part of makes me very proud. . . . When I was working on [the film] I was like, "This is the best job in the world!"[30]

As Minaj was wrapping up the Pink Friday: Reloaded Tour, she continued her media blitz by teasing a new album: "I'm putting lots of new songs on there and I'm actually going to drop my new single like next week. Barbz, you are gonna spaz. You are gonna love it. You are gonna go crazy!"[31] The songs were part of a November boxed set release, *Pink Friday: Roman Reloaded— The Re-Up*, an expanded version of the album Minaj released in April. *The Re-Up* consisted of three discs: one CD with seven new songs, a second CD of the original *Pink Friday* album, and a DVD that featured behind-the-scenes footage of Minaj working on the songs in the studio. The album received good reviews, but the reissue only rose to number twenty-seven on the *Billboard* 200.

Television Tantrums

Even as Minaj was promoting *The Re-Up*, talk of the album was overshadowed by gossip surrounding the upcoming twelfth season of *American Idol*. Minaj signed on as a judge on the talent show in September 2012. Other cast members included pop star Mariah Carey, country singer Keith Urban, and TV personality Randy Jackson. During filmed auditions, the two divas clashed after Carey bragged about her own accomplishments and interrupted Minaj on camera several times. After rumors spread about the hostility between the two judges, host Ryan Seacrest went on *The Today Show* to announce that everyone was getting along just fine.

Seacrest's soothing words were soon forgotten. While filming auditions in North Carolina, the rapper and the pop singer got in a fight over a contestant's performance. Minaj unleashed a string of obscenities directed at Carey. The event was captured on a shaky smartphone video that was leaked online and went viral. The day after the argument, Carey told TV host Barbara Walters that she was forced to hire extra security because the unpredictable Minaj threatened to shoot her. Minaj denied the allegation on Twitter: "Hey yAll. Let's just say Nick said [something] about a gun. ppl will believe it cuz [I'm] a black rapper. Lmao. . . . Ironically, no camera or mic heard the gun comment tho. Lol @ the struggle. Not even the producers believed u. Say no to violence barbz."[32] Several days later Carey and Minaj met with show producers to smooth things out. Minaj told Carey she loves her but they might fight again. Carey responded: "No, we will not."[33]

Carey was wrong. During live broadcasts in 2013, Minaj continually baited Carey. Minaj shamelessly flirted with male contestants, made crazy cartoon faces, spoke in a goofy British accent, and generally upstaged Carey at every opportunity. As television reviewer Lyndsey Parker wrote,

Mariah *really* felt threatened by Nicki's massive, scene-stealing, scenery-chewing [overacting] presence. Because honestly, when Nicki was on the screen . . . I barely noticed that Mariah, or anyone else, was even sitting at the judges' table. It was totally "The Nicki Minaj Show" up in there. And you know what? "The Nicki Minaj Show" was darn good TV.[34]

Nicki Minaj's appearance as one of the judges on American Idol resulted in controversy when her obscenity-laden spat with fellow judge Mariah Carey was caught on video and posted online.

Carey tried to fight back. During a May broadcast, she created tension by pointing out that she had a number one song on the charts at the time while Minaj did not. In the end, both divas decided that *American Idol* was doing nothing for their music careers. When the season was over, both announced they would not be returning the following year.

American Idol was not the only television show of 2012 featuring the scenery-chewing Minaj. In November the E! cable network aired a three-part documentary called *Nicki Minaj: My Truth*. Whereas Minaj projected a lovable image on *Idol*, often hugging and encouraging contestants, she came across as unlikable on *My Truth*. The series showed Minaj seesawing between a self-important, vain rapper and an insecure child who threw temper tantrums when things did not go perfectly.

Whatever the public thought of Minaj's television appearances, no one could argue that she was breaking one record after another with her music in 2013. At the end of the year, *Billboard* announced that Minaj had charted more singles on the Hot 100 than any other female rapper. With forty-four hits, Minaj tied

A clothing line called the Nicki Minaj Collection includes accessories such as bejeweled hats, gold chain necklaces, and patterned leggings.

with Carey for most singles by women in all genres. Minaj led all other rap musicians with seven nominations for *Billboard* Music Awards. She won the BET Award for Best Female Hip-Hop Artist in 2013 for the fourth consecutive year, another record. Minaj also found success in the fashion world, launching a fragrance called Minajesty and a clothing line called the Nicki Minaj Collection, which included accessories such as gold chain necklaces, patterned leggings, and bejeweled hats.

Personal Issues

With her successful ventures in retail and the entertainment industry, Minaj landed at number four on the 2013 *Forbes* magazine Hip-Hop Cash Kings list. Minaj was the first woman to make the list in 2011, and with a net worth of $29 million, she beat Kanye West, Lil Wayne, and Ludacris. Rapper Pharrell Williams summed up Minaj's success: "She's done everything and she's everywhere in a time frame that breaks every record. The only thing left is . . . inner. We know when she flexes there's nobody who can stand next to her. But talking to yourself is the next challenge."[35]

Williams's comment seemed prophetic in 2014 when Minaj was forced to deal with personal issues that required self-reflection. She ended a ten-year relationship with Safaree Samuels, a rapper she met after joining rap group the HoodStars in 2002. The couple had a turbulent relationship, made more difficult because Minaj felt the need to keep it secret. She recalls, "When I came in the business, you couldn't tell people you were in a relationship, because the record company and management said that doesn't make you appealing to men. So don't tell people you're in a relationship."[36] Additionally, Minaj's success made Samuels very jealous, creating additional conflict that led to the breakup.

"She's done everything and she's everywhere in a time frame that breaks every record. . . . We know when she flexes there's nobody who can stand next to her."[35]

—Pharrell Williams, rapper

Events in Minaj's turbulent life were described in detail on the tracks of her third studio album, *The Pinkprint*, released in December 2014. Minaj says she wanted to get back to her hip-hop roots on the new record after exploring dance-pop on her previous release. Like other Minaj albums, *The Pinkprint* featured collaborations galore, with appearances by Drake, Chris Brown, Skylar Grey, Ariana Grande, Beyoncé, and Lil Wayne.

Some of the tracks on *The Pinkprint* reflect on Minaj's pensive mood, dealing with her heartbreak as well as the abortion she had as a teenager. The lead single from the album, "Pills n Potions," is a bittersweet breakup ballad. Minaj sings and raps the song over a sparse, haunting piano and drum arrangement. Minaj describes the song: "It sounds like urgency. It sounds like betrayal. It sounds like running. It sounds like fainting. It sounds like love. It sounds like—*gasp!*"[37] On a slow-burning track called "The Crying Game," Minaj appears to be rapping directly to Samuels, seemingly blaming herself for the breakup.

Minaj understands that most hip-hop fans are not interested in sad rap songs. And *The Pinkprint* delivers the type of fist-pumping, X-rated hip-hop that placed her on the Hip Hop Cash Kings list. The songs and videos of "Anaconda" and "The Night Is Still Young" feature plenty of Barbz-friendly dancing, fashion, and shout-out choruses.

Minaj's roller-coaster personal life was further revealed in the 2014 MTV documentary *My Time Again*. The show portrays Minaj in moments of joy, such as watching the video for "Anaconda" drop. She is also seen in moments of despair, despondent about

Extravagant Concerts

Like almost every other Nicki Minaj project, the ninety-minute concerts on her Pink Friday Tour were unique and extravagant. Each show was divided into five acts, with DJs filling in the gaps between costume changes and set changes. The show began with Minaj dressed in a black cloak in a church-like setting, telling a story about her alter ego Roman, who traveled to planet Earth to defeat an evil force named Nemesis. Minaj then kicked up the energy, popping out the bars of "Roman's Revenge" or "Roman Holiday" surrounded by cape-clad dancers. Minaj shed her cloak to perform several hip-hop singles from *Pink Friday: Roman's Revenge* in a revealing pink and black polka-dot outfit.

During the second part of the show, Minaj played some of the mellower R&B ballads from the album before the third segment kicked off with the high-energy dance-pop "Starships" and "Sound the Alarm." For the fourth segment of the concert, Minaj took the stage in a confessional mood, talking to the audience about the anger she felt when an unnamed person—most likely ex-boyfriend Safaree Samuels—broke her heart. The last segment pushed the show into high gear as Minaj rapped songs from her earlier mixtapes, climaxing with megahits like "Super Bass" and "Monster."

an embarrassing appearance at the *MTV Video Music Awards*, where she experienced a wardrobe malfunction.

While Minaj had her emotional ups and downs, *The Pinkprint* was a triumph. The record debuted at number two on the *Billboard* 200 and was streamed nearly 17 million times the first week. In 2015 *Billboard* ranked *The Pinkprint* as the seventh most popular album of the year. While Minaj might have been an emotional wreck while making the record, her musical instincts did not fail. She took a deep dive into her innermost feelings and channeled her grief into a double platinum album that *Rolling Stone* ranked third on its 40 Best Rap Albums of 2014 list.

In 2015 Minaj played her third concert tour, the Pinkprint Tour, which earned over $22 million from sold-out shows in Europe and North America. By this time Minaj had accomplished more in three years than some rappers do during their entire careers. She played to the biggest crowds, sold the most records, and made a splash on screens large and small. She might have experienced some heartrending setbacks, but the Nicki Minaj Show—in all its forms—kept on moving forward to a beat that was hers and hers alone.

THE CONTROVERSIAL QUEEN BEE

Nicki Minaj has always been the author of her own story. When she was young she constructed an imaginary world in which she was rich and powerful. Today that fantasy is reality—Minaj is the queen, while her fanatical fans, the Barbz, are her loyal subjects. Outside of the concert hall, Minaj's realm exists online, made up of her 21 million Twitter followers. Fans also run Twitter sites like Nicki Daily, which boasted more than a quarter million followers in 2019.

The Barbz have an outsized presence in Minaj's digital queendom. Their social media handles relate to Minaj's songs, albums, and alter egos. Barbz bios often list the exact time and date their "Minajesty" decided to follow them back. The Barbz band together whenever Minaj drops a new song or album, using their collective purchasing power to drive the release up the iTunes music charts. And the Barbz act as palace guards if anyone criticizes Minaj. As music journalist Charles Holmes explains, "If Nicki is their queen bee, each [one of the Barbz] is a buzzing worker bee intent on protecting her majesty at any cost. No jab, swipe or Twitter critique escapes their purview."[38]

The Barbz are always ready to fight what they describe as the "Nicki hate train."[39] This train includes music journalists, bloggers, other rappers, and average hip-hop fans who do not loyally praise Minaj or recognize her many accomplishments. Hip-hop journalist Wanna Thompson stirred up the wrath of the Barbz with a single tweet in 2018: "You know how dope it would be if Nicki put out mature content. No sil-

ly [stuff], just reflecting on past rela-
tionships, being a boss, hardships,
etc. She's touching 40 soon. New
direction is needed."[40] Minaj, who
was thirty-five at the time, tweeted an insulting, obscenity-laced
rant in reply. Thompson's life was
turned upside down as thousands
of Barbz clapped back. They sent vi-
cious tweets to Thompson and even left
threatening messages on her personal cell
phone. While the Barbz were enraged, some wondered whether
Thompson's message hit too close to home. Did Minaj need to
find a new, more mature direction?

> "If Nicki is their queen bee,
> each [one of the Barbz] is a
> buzzing worker bee intent
> on protecting her majesty
> at any cost. No jab, swipe
> or Twitter critique escapes
> their purview."[38]
>
> —Charles Holmes, music journalist

Proving Herself Again

Minaj hardly seems to need defending. In 2017 she hit another milestone in her career after simultaneously releasing three
singles, "Changed It," "Regret in Your Tears," and "No Frauds"
(with Drake and Lil Wayne). Each song entered the *Billboard*
Hot 100 chart, giving Minaj a career total of seventy-six Hot
100 hits. With this accomplishment, Minaj had charted more
singles on the Hot 100 than any other female artist. She broke
the forty-year record held by soul singer Aretha Franklin, who
had seventy-three Hot 100 singles. The achievement also put
Minaj ahead of pop stars Taylor Swift, Rihanna, Madonna, and
Beyoncé.

Despite her success, Minaj was facing new competition
in 2018 as she prepared to release her fourth studio album,
Queen. Rapper Cardi B had burst onto the scene in 2017 with
the release of her megahit single "Bodak Yellow," and some reviewers were calling her the next Nicki Minaj. And it had been
four years since the release of Minaj's last album, *The Pinkprint*.
Expectations were high, and as Minaj in an October 2017 interview, she knew she had to prove herself once again: "I had so

much going against me in the beginning; being black, being a woman, being a female rapper. No matter how many times I get on a track with everyone's favorite M.C. and hold my own, [hip-hop] culture never seems to want to give me my props as an M.C., as a lyricist, as a writer. I got to prove myself a hundred times."[41]

In April 2018 Minaj proved herself again. She dropped a pair of lead singles from *Queen* on the same day. The songs, "Chun-Li" and "Barbie Tingz," were released on the tenth anniversary of Minaj's second mixtape, *Sucka Free*. The name "Chun-Li" is taken from a character in the Japanese video game

> "[Hip-hop] culture never seems to want to give me my props as an M.C., as a lyricist, as a writer. I got to prove myself a hundred times."[41]
>
> —Nicki Minaj

Street Fighter. The choice is appropriate, since Minaj furiously spews out the song's bars with the anger of a 1990s hard-core gangsta rapper. She skewers unnamed enemies, accuses them of stealing her words, and promises to thump her chest in victory like the enormous movie ape King Kong. Reviewers and fans alike were thrilled with Minaj's return to intense, hard-core hip-hop. "Chun-Li" quickly climbed to number ten on the Hot 100. "Barbie Tingz" covered similar lyrical and musical themes as "Chun-Li" but was not as well received, peaking at number twenty-five.

Queen was released in August 2018, and the rap-oriented album featured guest appearances by pop and hip-hop royalty,

The Nicki Daily Twitter Account

Nicki Minaj has 21 million followers on Twitter. And some of her most fanatical fans, the Barbz, create their own Twitter accounts in order to defend Minaj and help her promote her work. A site called Nicki Daily, founded by a dedicated fan known as Nick, had more than 267,000 Twitter followers in 2019. Nick explains why the Barbz are so quick to clap back at anyone who criticizes Minaj:

I don't go as hard as some people do. . . . [But some Barbz] feel like people don't give [Minaj] the credit that they [think] she deserves, for all of her hard work. . . . So I think as fans we get frustrated and so we have to go out and try to prove to people you know exactly what kind of person she is, her accomplishments. . . . I feel like the type of artist that she is and the type of person that she is I really admire and respect and she's really inspired me. . . . I feel like I'm helping out with her and her brand, and help promoting her, and things like that. I try to be a positive influence when it comes to her, cause I feel like she does deserve that. She just really inspires me in life.

Quoted in Charles Holmes, "Meet the Barbz: The Nicki Minaj Fandom Fighting the 'Nicki Hate Train,'" *Rolling Stone*, August 1, 2018. www.rollingstone.com.

including Lil Wayne, Eminem, Ariana Grande, the Weeknd, Future, and Foxy Brown. And the number of rappers and pop stars Minaj disrespected on the album was even larger than those who appeared as guests. In a single song, "Barbie Dreams," Minaj recites wickedly funny bars dissing Cardi B, Meek Mill, Drake, Lil Uzi Vert, Young Thug, DJ Khaled, and 50 Cent. Some of those mentioned were not thrilled to be in Minaj's crosshairs; Cardi B only found out she was mentioned in "Barbie Dreams" when her name began trending on Twitter. Others, such as Drake, one of Minaj's oldest friends, took the diss in good humor.

Whatever the individual reactions, Minaj said the lyrics of "Barbie Dreams" were meant to be playful and fun. She might have added that the diss track was a smart business move. As journalist Ben Beaumont-Thomas points out, "[The song 'Bar-

Nicki Minaj and Ariana Grande perform at the MTV Video Music Awards in 2016. Grande was one of a number of pop and hip-hop stars who appeared on Minaj's 2018 album, Queen.

bie Dreams'] is the perfect track for a gossipy, meme-obsessed age, and Minaj smartly puts herself at the front of the social media conversation."[42] That controversial social media conversation helped push "Barbie Dreams" to number eighteen on the Hot 100 when the song was released two days after *Queen* dropped.

Ruler of the Radio

Minaj occasionally put aside her verbal flamethrower for rap ballads like "Come See About Me." But she remained the undisputed empress of hip-hop. Tracks on *Queen* are filled with razor-sharp, tongue-twisting lines delivered in a range of vocal twangs that prove Minaj has little competition as an emcee, lyricist, and writer. As journalist Briana Younger writes, "[On *Queen*] Nicki jettisons all the . . . madness [and] drowns out the noise. . . . Never lacking for charisma and attitude, her flows and cadences are a whirlwind of husky aggression and bouncing animation. She sends shots in every direction . . . with the confidence of a woman holding court in a kingdom she conquered."[43]

"[Nicki's] flows and cadences are a whirlwind of husky aggression and bouncing animation. She sends shots in every direction . . . with the confidence of a woman holding court in a kingdom she conquered."[43]

—Briana Younger, journalist

Queen conquered the charts, debuting at number two on the *Billboard* 200. And the album charted in the top ten in the United Kingdom, Australia, Canada, the Netherlands, New Zealand, and elsewhere. The video of "Chun-Li" won the Best Hip-Hop Video prize at the 2018 *MTV Video Music Awards*, and by 2019 the video had racked up nearly 125 million YouTube views.

In coordination with the album's release, Minaj launched the *Queen Radio* show on Beats 1, a streaming service of Apple Music. Fourteen episodes of *Queen Radio* were aired intermittently from August 2018 to June 2019. On the first episode, Minaj ran through the *Queen* album track by track, explaining the meaning and the message behind the lyrics. She began subsequent episodes by reading her favorite fan tweets, followed by phone calls from Barbz who wanted unfiltered advice about their sex lives. Minaj also played her favorite songs by other artists and conducted interviews with pop stars and celebrities, including Alicia Keys, Kim Kardashian, Lil Wayne, Tyga, Trina, and Soulja Boy. *Queen Radio* quickly became the most popular program on Beats 1, and Minaj enjoyed the role of radio DJ.

Reaching Out to a New Generation

Minaj used *Queen Radio* to promote her recent collaborations with up-and-coming rappers such as 6ix9ine, a newcomer who became instantly famous in late 2017 after releasing the track "Gummo" on the music-sharing website SoundCloud. 6ix9ine was as well known for his candy-colored dreadlocks and multicolored tooth caps as he was for his aggressive rap style. But in 2018 Minaj was taking steps to reach out to up-and-coming artists—and their audiences—so she collaborated with 6ix9ine on his hit single "Fefe."

Minaj checked in with the new generation of South Korean pop stars when she appeared on the single "Idol" by the K-pop boy band BTS. If any act generated more tweets, downloads, video views, or legions of rabid fans than Minaj, it would be BTS. While the group had been stars in South Korea since 2013, BTS became one of the biggest bands in the world in 2018. When "Idol" was released in late August, several days after *Queen* dropped, the BTS single hit the top ten. This gave Minaj her second top ten hit in a month. The video of "Idol" rocketed to the top of YouTube's trending list and attracted a record 27 million views in around eight hours.

Minaj and BTS might seem like an unlikely pairing, but the acts share a number of musical and visual styles. Like Minaj, BTS mixes gangster rap (in Korean) with dance-pop, voice synthesizers, colorful costumes, and exhilarating dance routines. But the Minaj-BTS collaboration illuminated the shifting musical tastes of the American public. A few years earlier, it would have been a major score for BTS to work with an artist of Minaj's stature. But in 2018 BTS was so popular that the musical alliance boosted Minaj's profile by exposing her music to a younger, international K-pop audience that might not have previously followed her career.

Minaj might have been looking to further enhance her international visibility when she made an October 2018 guest appearance on the song "Woman like Me" by the British girl group Little Mix. While many of Minaj's American fans might not be familiar with Little Mix, the quartet's blend of R&B and dance-pop is incredibly popular in the United Kingdom, where they are the best-selling girl group of all time. "Woman like Me" mixes tight harmonies and Jamaican reggae rhythms with a memorable chorus. Minaj rap-sings the third verse in her unique sassy style, supplying some hip-hop credibility to what might be considered an otherwise lightweight pop song. "Woman like Me" reached number two in the United Kingdom, number three in Ireland, and number four on the *Billboard* Bubbling Under Hot 100 chart, which lists

Members of the South Korean boy band BTS pose with their trophy at the Mnet Asian Music Awards in 2018. Nicki Minaj's appearance—just a few days after the release of Queen—on BTS's single, "Idol," became her second top ten hit in a month.

popular songs that have not yet charted on the Hot 100. The video, which features the scantily clad Minaj as a painting come to life, won British Artist Video of the Year at the 2019 Brit Awards.

Rivalries and Controversies

Like some other recent Minaj projects, the "Woman like Me" collaboration was accompanied by a social media meltdown that attracted nearly as much attention as the music. The conflict over the song began when Cardi B claimed on Instagram that she had been asked first to appear on "Woman like Me." Cardi B said she turned down the request because she was busy working on her own songs. Little Mix jumped into the fray, tweeting that their record label offered both rappers a chance to appear on the song but they always admired Minaj and wanted to work with her.

While the Cardi B fracas attracted a lot of attention, it was only one of several negative events that overshadowed Minaj's music in 2018. Minaj was criticized for collaborating with 6ix9ine after it was revealed that he had been arrested in 2015 for shooting a video that showed a thirteen-year-old girl in a sexual situation. Minaj defended her actions on Twitter but later deleted the tweets.

Minaj generated more controversy in 2019 after she agreed to play the Jeddah World Fest in Saudi Arabia. Minaj would have had a huge payday from the gig; she was scheduled to be the headlining act in a show that would be broadcast globally. After the show was announced, Minaj was widely criticized. Human rights activists pointed out that Saudi Arabia is a repressive kingdom that denies women equal rights and routinely arrests and executes gays and lesbians. Others had recently played in Saudi Arabia, including Mariah Carey, Steve Aoki, and Sean Paul. Few can resist the exorbitant sums the oil-rich kingdom pays popular music acts. But after the negative publicity, Minaj decided to cancel her appearance. As she said in a statement to the Associated Press, "While I want nothing more than to bring my show to fans in Saudi Arabia, after better educating myself on the issues, I believe it is important for me to make clear my support for the rights of women, the LGBTQ community and freedom of expression."[44]

Nicki Minaj vs. Cardi B

Many rappers keep their names trending on social media by engaging in online "rap battles" with competitors. This not only keeps fans engaged but also helps sell records and merchandise. And like most of Nicki Minaj's other efforts, her rap battles are epic. Minaj's most famous beef was with Cardi B. The two had been rivals since 2017, when Cardi B became the first female rapper to simultaneously have two number one hits on the Hot 100, something Minaj never accomplished. In September 2018 sparks flew when Minaj and Cardi B attended the *Harper's Bazaar* Fashion Week party in New York City. The two rappers engaged in a heated verbal exchange. A viral video shows Cardi B lunging at Minaj and throwing a shoe at her. Cardi B, who had recently given birth, said Minaj questioned her mothering skills. Security pinned the fight on Cardi B, who was escorted out of the event— barefoot and with a bump on her head. Minaj later denied saying anything about Cardi B's newborn daughter and called the altercation mortifying. Minaj kept the rap beef alive after the event by making numerous derogatory remarks about Cardi B on *Queen Radio*, and the feud continued with no end in sight.

New Boyfriend, New Criticism

After the social media storm surrounding Cardi B and 6ix9ine, Minaj kept a relatively low profile, staying off Twitter for nearly three months. She broke her silence in June 2019, tweeting a single cryptic word: "MEGATRON."[45] This got the Barbz buzzing as rumors flew that Minaj was about to drop another album. But fan expectations did not fit with Minaj's typical timeline. She usually spreads out her releases by several years, promoting each album while working on the next offering. It had only been a year since *Queen* dropped. But fans speculated that after working with SoundCloud rappers and a K-pop band, Minaj might be bending to the demands of the modern marketplace; music fans expect a constant stream of new music from their favorite artists.

Rumors were put to rest when Minaj released the single "Megatron" several weeks after the tweet. Despite the hate train that had been speeding along for months, the song was another record-setting success. The dance hall–style song floats along on electrified Caribbean rhythms as Minaj lays down bars comparing herself to the character Megatron from the *Transformers* movie franchise. Fans were eager for new Minaj music, and "Megatron" debuted at number twenty on the Hot 100. "Megatron" extended Minaj's record for the most entries on the chart and helped her achieve another milestone: she broke the record for the most top twenty hits for a female artist in the 2010s.

While racking up records, "Megatron" brought a fresh eruption of criticism. The single arrived with the "Megatron" music video that showed Minaj in a number of steamy scenes with her latest boyfriend, Kenneth "Zoo" Petty. It did not take long for critics to discover that the forty-year-old Petty, who works in the music industry, is a registered sex offender with an extensive rap sheet. Petty was convicted of first-degree attempted rape when he was sixteen. He also served time for first-degree manslaughter in connection with the shooting death of a man in 2002. But as a Queens native, Petty had a hometown connection with Minaj. Some of the Barbz were up in arms over Minaj's new man and left hundreds of comments on her Instagram page. Minaj clapped back, essentially telling them to get a life, before she disabled the "Megatron" comments section.

Fans were stung again in September 2019 when Minaj tweeted she was retiring from the music business. She said she was going to marry Petty and start a family. The next day Minaj deleted the tweet and apologized for being abrupt and insensitive. However, Minaj never clarified what her true plans might be, leaving the Barbz in suspense. With a net worth of $85 million, Minaj is in a position to do whatever she pleases. In 2019 she remained the first female rapper to sell over 5 million copies of each of her albums and has charted more than double the number of singles that Michael Jackson charted in his lifetime. Backed by the Barbz, Minaj became a household name in little more than a decade. With powerful words, a hard-hitting personality, and a photogenic physique, Minaj cut all critics and remained on top. Even if the queen steps away from her throne, the reign of Nicki Minaj will not soon be forgotten.

Introduction: Spearheading a Movement

1. Quoted in Susannah Breslin, "Nicki Minaj Battles Hip-Hop's Heavy Hitters for Booze Supremacy," *Forbes*, June 15, 2013. www.forbes.com.
2. Quoted in Joshua Espinoza, "Nicki Minaj to Those Who Have Questioned Her Success: 'I'ma Call Y'all Out One by One,'" *Complex*, July 5, 2019. www.complex.com.
3. Quoted in Nerisha Penrose, "Nicki Minaj Calls Out Sexism in Hip-Hop on Twitter," *Billboard*, October 26, 2017. www.billboard.com.
4. Quoted in Hermione Hoby, "Nicki Minaj: 'I Am Doing Everything the Boys Can—Plus More,'" *Guardian* (Manchester), November 27, 2010. www.theguardian.com.

Chapter One: The Rap Queen of Queens

5. Quoted in Renee Cummings, "Carol Maraj—Mother of Hip Hop Star Nicki Minaj," *Trinidad Express* (Port of Spain, Trinidad and Tobago), July 21, 2012. www.trinidadexpress.com.
6. Quoted in Siobhan O'Connor, "Character Study: Just How Real Is Nicki Minaj?," *Vibe*, June 23, 2010. www.vibe.com.
7. Quoted in Brian Hiatt, "Nicki Minaj: The New Queen of Hip-Hop," *Rolling Stone*, December 9, 2010. www.rollingstone.com.
8. Quoted in Hiatt, "Nicki Minaj."
9. Quoted in Judith Newman, "Nicki Minaj: Her *Allure* Photo Shoot," *Allure*, March 13, 2012. www.allure.com.
10. Quoted in O'Connor, "Character Study."
11. Quoted in O'Connor, "Character Study."
12. Quoted in O'Connor, "Character Study."
13. Quoted in Jason S. Lipshutz, "Nicki Minaj Catches Eyes on Lil Wayne's Young Money Tour," *Billboard*, August 10, 2009. www.billboard.com.

Chapter Two: In the Pink

14. Aaron Williams, "Nicki Minaj Proved She's Worthy of Her Throne with the Lyrically-Focused 'Beam Me Up Scotty,'" Uproxx, August 23, 2018. https://uproxx.com.

15. Allison P. Davis, "Every Rap Song That Mentions Monica Le-winsky," *The Cut* (blog), *New York*, March 24, 2015. www .thecut.com.

16. Quoted in Shaheem Reid, "Lil Wayne Introduces Nicki Minaj," MTV, May 1, 2009. www.mtv.com.

17. Williams, "Nicki Minaj Proved She's Worthy of Her Throne with the Lyrically-Focused 'Beam Me Up Scotty.'"

18. Williams, "Nicki Minaj Proved She's Worthy of Her Throne with the Lyrically-Focused 'Beam Me Up Scotty.'"

19. Quoted in Hiatt, "Nicki Minaj."

20. Quoted in Mariel Concepcion, "Nicki Minaj: The *Billboard* Cover Story," *Billboard*, November 12, 2010. www.billboard .com.

21. Quoted in Maura Johnson, "Nicki Minaj's Much-Anticipated 'Pink Friday' Leaks," *Rolling Stone*, November 17, 2010. www.rollingstone.com.

22. Quoted in D.L. Chandler, "Nicki Minaj 'Letting It All Hang Out' on 'Super Bass' Video Set," MTV, March 3, 2010. www.mtv .com.

23. Quoted in Hiatt, "Nicki Minaj."

24. Quoted in Hiatt, "Nicki Minaj."

Chapter Three: Racking Up Records

25. Quoted in Latifah Muhammad, "Nicki Minaj Excited About New Single, Talks Super Bowl Performance, M.I.A. Flipping the Bird," Hip-Hop Wired, February 14, 2012. https://hiphop wired.com.

26. Quoted in "Nicki Minaj: 'Roman Reloaded' Represents 'Free-dom,'" Rap-Up, March 6, 2012. www.rap-up.com.

27. Jody Rosen, "*Pink Friday: Roman Reloaded*," *Rolling Stone*, April 6, 2012. www.rollingstone.com.

28. Jon Caramanica, "A Stylish Assassin Shows a Softer Side," *New York Times*, July 17, 2012. www.nytimes.com.

29. Quoted in N. Campbell, "Nicki Minaj Talks Her First Big Tour, Big Surprise for Fans," Urban Islandz, June 29, 2012. https:// urbanislandz.com.

30. Quoted in Justin Harp, "Nicki Minaj: 'Ice Age 4 Is a Blessing and an Honour,'" Digital Spy, April 7, 2012. www.digitalspy .com.

31. Quoted in Rap-Up, "Nicki Minaj Readies 'Roman Reloaded—the Re-Up' for November," September 7, 2012. www.rap-up.com.
32. Quoted in *Rolling Stone*, "Nicki Minaj Fires Back on Twitter After Mariah Carey Alleges Threats," October 4, 2012. www.rollingstone.com.
33. Quoted in *Rolling Stone*, "Nicki Minaj Fires Back on Twitter After Mariah Carey Alleges Threats."
34. Lyndsey Parker, "'American Idol' Preview: Season 12 Just May Be 'the Nicki Minaj Show,'" *Rolling Stone*, January 14, 2013. www.rollingstone.com.
35. Quoted in Miss Info, "Nicki Minaj: Self-Possessed," *Complex*, March 20, 2012. www.complex.com.
36. Quoted in Shawn Setaro, "A Timeline of Nicki Minaj and Safaree's Relationship," *Complex*, August 15, 2018. www.complex.com.
37. Quoted in Chris Payne, "Nicki Minaj Drops 'Pills n Potions,' Her New Dr. Luke-Produced Single," *Billboard*, May 21, 2014. www.billboard.com.

Chapter Four: The Controversial Queen Bee

38. Charles Holmes, "Meet the Barbz: The Nicki Minaj Fandom Fighting the 'Nicki Hate Train,'" *Rolling Stone*, August 1, 2018. www.rollingstone.com.
39. Quoted in Holmes, "Meet the Barbz."
40. Quoted in Holmes, "Meet the Barbz."
41. Quoted in Sarah Jasmine Montgomery, "Nicki Minaj Is One of the Greats," *Fader*, October 16, 2017. www.thefader.com.
42. Ben Beaumont-Thomas, "Nicki Minaj: Queen Review—Uneasy Coronation for Rap's Manic Monarch," *Guardian* (Manchester), August 13, 2018. www.theguardian.com.
43. Briana Younger, "Nicki Minaj: Queen," Pitchfork, August 14, 2018. https://pitchfork.com.
44. Quoted in Helena Andrews-Dyer, "Nicki Minaj Pulls Out of Concert in Saudi Arabia 'After Better Educating Myself on the Issues,'" *Washington Post*, July 9, 2019. www.washingtonpost.com.
45. Quoted in Michael Saponara, "Nicki Minaj Returns with Cryptic 'Megatron' Tweet," *Billboard*, June 12, 2019., www.billboard.com.

Important Events in the Life of Nicki Minaj

1982

Nicki Minaj is born Onika Tanya Maraj on December 8.

1988

Five-year-old Nicki moves from Trinidad to Queens, New York, to join her parents.

1996

Minaj attends Fiorello H. LaGuardia High School of Music & Art and Performing Arts in Manhattan.

2002

Minaj joins rap group the HoodStars.

2007

Minaj releases her first mixtape, *Playtime Is Over*, with a guest appearance by superstar rapper Lil Wayne.

2008

Sucka Free, Minaj's second mixtape, is released.

2009

Minaj drops her third mixtape, *Beam Me Up Scotty*, which features guest appearances by Drake, Lil Wayne, and others.

2010

Minaj releases her first studio album, *Pink Friday*, which debuts at number two on the *Billboard* 200 album chart.

2011

Minaj receives three Grammy Award nominations: Best New Artist, Best Rap Performance by a Duo or Group, and Best Rap Album.

2012

Minaj's second studio album, *Pink Friday: Roman Reloaded*, is released to universal acclaim.

2013

With a net worth of $29 million, Minaj is listed at number four on the *Forbes* Hip Hop Cash Kings list.

2014

Minaj's third studio album, *The Pinkprint*, is released.

2015

With sold-out shows in Europe and North America, Minaj's Pinkprint Tour earns over $22 million.

2017

With her seventy-sixth career hit on the *Billboard* Hot 100, Minaj sets a record for the most singles charted by a female artist.

2018

Minaj drops her fourth studio album, *Queen*, which debuts at number two on the *Billboard* 200.

2019

The single "Megatron" enters the *Billboard* top twenty; Minaj breaks the record for the most top twenty hits for a female artist in the 2010s; the singer announces plans to retire and start a family.

Books

Audrey Deangelis and Gina Deangelis, *Hip-Hop Dance*. Minneapolis, MN: Essential Library, 2017.

Stuart A. Kallen, *Rap and Hip-Hop*. San Diego, CA: ReferencePoint, 2020.

Joe L. Morgan, *Cardi B*. Broomall, PA: Mason Crest, 2018.

New York Times Editorial Staff, *Influential Hip-Hop Artists: Kendrick Lamar, Nicki Minaj, and Others*. New York: New York Times Educational, 2018.

Vanessa Oswald, *Hip-Hop: A Cultural and Musical Revolution*. New York: Lucent, 2019.

Internet Sources

Joe Coscarelli, "How One Tweet About Nicki Minaj Spiraled into Internet Chaos," *New York Times*, July 10, 2018. www.nytimes.com.

Charles Holmes, "Meet the Barbz: The Nicki Minaj Fandom Fighting the 'Nicki Hate Train,'" *Rolling Stone*, August 1, 2018. www.rollingstone.com.

Jiggy Jones, "How Hip-Hop's Transcending Influence Continues to Grow," The Source, February 2, 2018. http://thesource.com.

Sowmya Krishnamurthy, "Nicki Minaj Is the 21st Century's Insatiable Hip-Hop Monarch," NPR, October 3, 2018. www.npr.org.

Aaron Williams, "Nicki Minaj Proved She's Worthy of Her Throne with the Lyrically-Focused 'Beam Me Up Scotty,'" Uproxx, August 23, 2018. https://uproxx.com.